Boxcar Sleepover

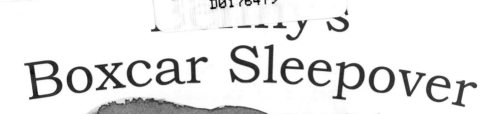

CREATED BY
Gertrude Chandler Warner

ILLUSTRATED BY
Kay Life

Albert Whitman & Company

Morton Grove, Illinois

You will also want to read:

Meet the Boxcar Children

A Present for Grandfather

Benny's New Friend

The Magic Show Mystery

Benny Goes into Business

Watch Runs Away

The Secret under the Tree

Benny's Saturday Surprise

Sam Makes Trouble

Watch, the Superdog!

Keys and Clues for Benny

Library of Congress Cataloging-in-Publication Data
Warner, Gertrude Chandler, 1890-1979
Benny's boxcar sleepover / created by Gertrude Chandler Warner ;
illustrated by Kay Life.
p. cm. — (The adventures of Benny and Watch ; #12)
Summary: Benny is excited about having his first sleepover,
but he and his friends are a little bit scared, too.
ISBN 0-8075-0636-2 (pbk.)
[1. Sleepovers—Fiction. 2. Fear of the dark—Fiction.] I. Life, Kay, ill. II. Title.
PZ7.W244Bm 2004   [E]—dc22 2004001690

Text copyright © 2004 by Albert Whitman & Company.
Illustrations copyright © 2004 by Kay Life.
Published in 2004 by Albert Whitman & Company,
6340 Oakton Street, Morton Grove, Illinois 60053.
Published simultaneously in Canada by Fitzhenry & Whiteside, Markham, Ontario.

Printed in the United States of America.
10 9 8 7 6 5 4 3 2 1

Henry

Violet

Jessie

Grandfather

Watch

Benny

The Boxcar Children

Henry, Jessie, Violet, and Benny Alden are orphans. They are supposed to live with their grandfather, but they have heard that he is mean.

So the children run away and live in an old red boxcar. They find a dog, and Benny names him Watch.

When Grandfather finds them, the children see that he is not mean at all. They happily go to live with him. And, as a surprise, Grandfather brings the boxcar along!

It was Saturday afternoon, but Benny Alden was not happy.

"Everyone has something fun to do tonight," he told Watch. "Henry will be working on his computer.

Violet and Jessie are sleeping over
with their friends. And Grandfather
is going out for dinner. It's just you
and me tonight, Watch."

Henry saw that Benny was sad. He decided to change his plans. "We could have that boxcar sleepover tonight," said Henry.

"Are you kidding?" asked Benny. Benny wanted to have a boxcar sleepover more than anything.

Henry laughed. "I'm not kidding. I'll help. Go call Michael and Tyler."

Benny made
two quick phone
calls. "They can
come!" he told
Henry.

"Okay," said
Henry. "No one will
get scared, will they? It gets pretty
dark in the boxcar at night."

Benny hadn't thought about being
scared. "No way," he said. At least
he didn't *think* that would happen.

Henry and Benny went to the grocery store to get some food for the sleepover.

"Let's get hot dogs," said Benny. "And pizza!" he added. "Better get some peanut butter, too."

Henry laughed. "I don't think we'll need that much." But he put it all in the cart, anyway. Then they got some chips, apples, and cookies.

They were putting the groceries away when a car pulled up. Michael and Tyler got out. They had sleeping bags, pillows, and duffel bags.

"I brought my new football," said Michael.

"I brought checkers," said Tyler. Benny was so excited. A real sleepover party at last! Michael's mother, Mrs. Hatch, said, "Call me if anyone gets scared."

There was that word again. *Scared…*

"What do you want for dinner?" Henry asked.

"Hot dogs!" all three shouted.

While Henry cooked the hot dogs, the boys tossed around Michael's new football.

"I don't think I'll get scared,"
said Benny.

"I won't if you won't," said Tyler.

"Only bears scare me,"
said Michael. "There aren't
any bears around here!"

After dinner, the boys were stuffed. As they started to clean up, Grandfather came home.

"Hi, boys," he said. "I heard about your sleepover and got something for you." He handed each boy, even Henry, a brand-new flashlight.

"Thanks!" said the boys as they
clicked the flashlights on and off.

"Just in case you get a little
scared," said Grandfather.

"Not us," said Michael.

"No way," said Tyler.

"I definitely won't get scared," said
Henry. "Now, how about I take you
three and Watch in a game of soccer?"

"Let's go!" said Benny.

They played three games, and Henry lost all three. Even Watch scored a goal.

"It's starting to get dark," said Henry. "Let's get settled in the boxcar."

The boys brushed their teeth and climbed into the boxcar. After they got into their sleeping bags, Henry started to tell a story. "In the dark woods lived a bear—" he began.

"A bear?" said Michael, sitting up. The other boys sat up, too. They clicked on their flashlights.

"Maybe a different story would be better," said Benny.

"Good idea," said Henry. "I'll tell about our championship game."

"Any bears in it?" asked Tyler.

"No, just baseball," promised Henry.

After the story, Henry said it was time for bed. The boys turned off their flashlights.

"Goodnight," said Michael.

"'Night," said Tyler, yawning.

But after one minute, Benny put his flashlight back on.

"What's wrong?" asked Henry.

"I have to go to the bathroom," said Benny.

"Me, too," said Michael.

"We'll all go," said Henry.

They climbed out of the boxcar.

"It's dark out here," said Tyler.

They all clutched their flashlights. They took one step— and heard a crash! Benny grabbed Henry's arm.

"What was that?" whispered Michael.

"I think it's a bear!" said Tyler.

"It came from over there," said Henry. He pointed his flashlight at some trash cans. The boys did the same. They saw something furry— but small.

"Just a raccoon!" said Benny. Everyone laughed and hurried into the house.

"Lights out," said Henry, when they got back to the boxcar.

"Now we can get some sleep," said Michael.

" 'Night," yawned Benny.

But now something was
scratching on the boxcar door.
Scratch,
    scratch,
       scratch.

The boys flashed on their lights.
"What's that?" Henry whispered.
"A bear?" said Michael.
"Or the raccoon?" asked Tyler.
"I don't like raccoons too much."

They heard the noise again. *Scratch, scratch, scratch.* Then they heard a whimper. Benny knew that sound!

"That's no bear," he said. "Open the door, Henry!"

Henry did, and in jumped Watch! The boys laughed as Watch ran around wagging his tail.

"I guess Watch just wanted to join the sleepover," said Benny.

"Okay," said Henry, "this time we are really going to sleep."

The next morning, Grandfather made pancakes for the boys.

"My stomach is growling," said Benny as they sat down to eat.

"How'd it go?" said Grandfather. "Did anyone get scared?"

The boys looked at each other.
Henry said, "Well, I got a little
scared. But everyone else was fine."
Michael and Tyler smiled.
Benny winked at Henry and said,
"Watch helped protect us!"

"Woof!" agreed Watch.